10 Minutes to
SHOWTIME

10 Minutes to
SHOWTIME

By Tricia Goyer
Illustrations by Maryn Roos

Tommy NELSON®
www.tommynelson.com
A Division of Thomas Nelson, Inc.
www.ThomasNelson.com

Library of Congress Cataloging-in-Publication Data

Goyer, Tricia.
  10 minutes to showtime! / by Tricia Goyer ; illustrations by Maryn
Roos.
      p. cm.
  Summary: A group of angels behind a curtain in the sky prepares for a
big debut over the manger in Bethlehem.
  ISBN 1-4003-0470-9 (hardcover)
  1. Jesus Christ—Nativity—Juvenile fiction. [1. Jesus
Christ—Nativity—Fiction. 2. Angels—Fiction.] I. Title: Ten minutes
to showtime!. II. Roos, Maryn, ill. III. Title.
  PZ7.G7483Aae 2004
  [E]--dc22

                            2004010964

Printed in the United States of America
04 05 06 07 LBM 5 4 3 2 1

To my children, Cory, Leslie, and Nathan,
who opened my eyes to the wonder of Christmas.

Mommy loves you.

"10 minutes to showtime!"

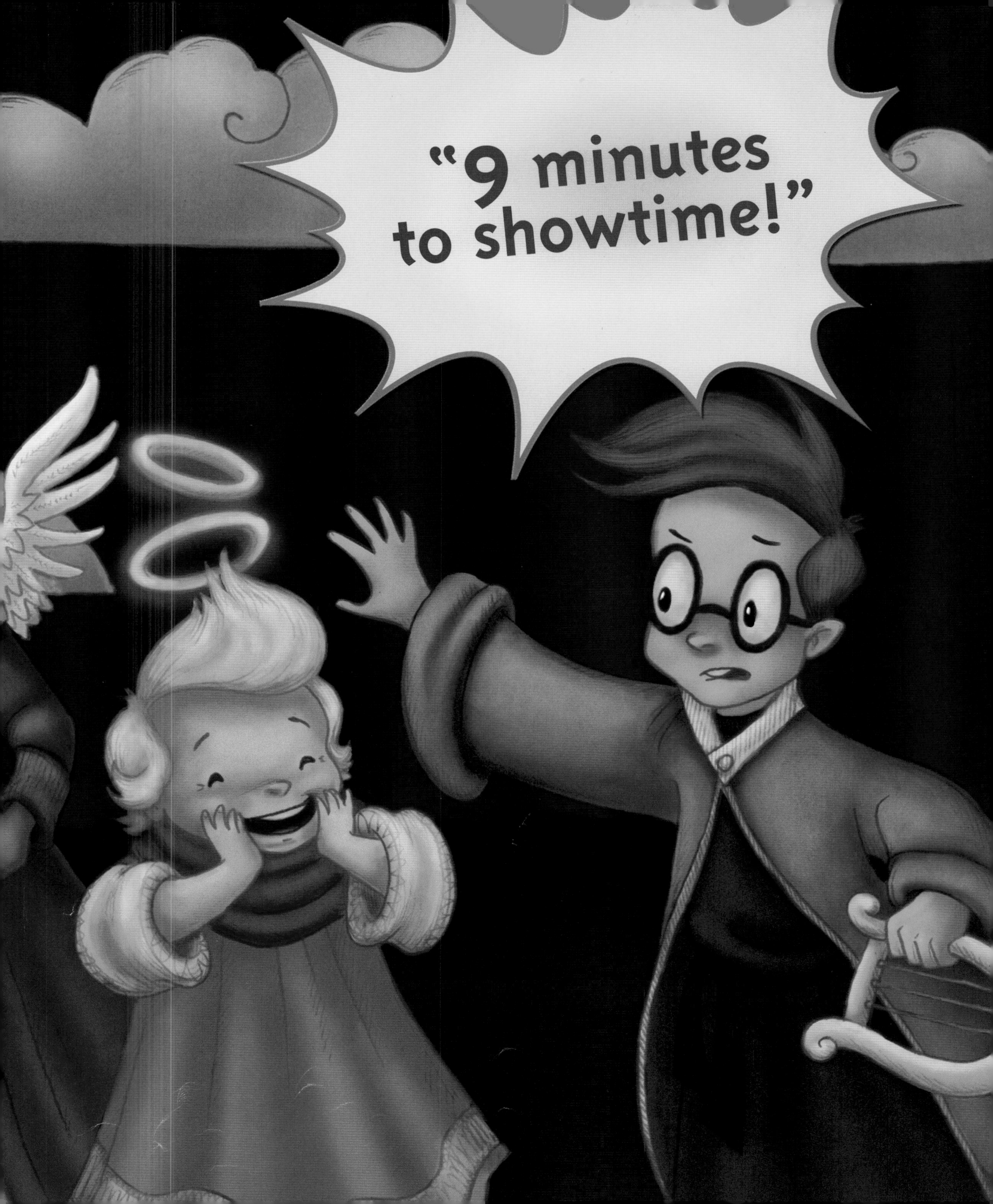
"9 minutes to showtime!"

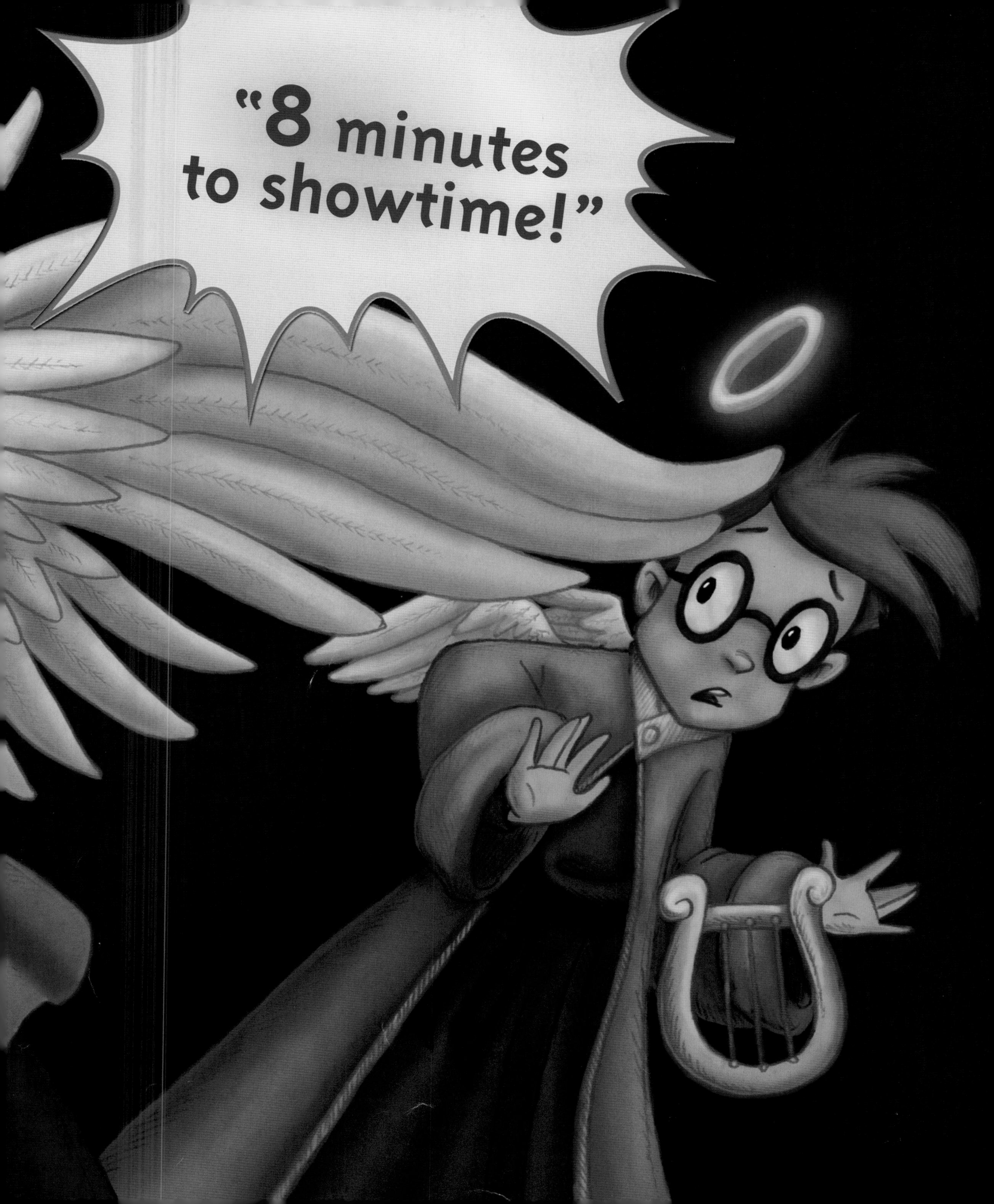
"8 minutes to showtime!"

Man, those lights are bright!

"Just wait. . . ."

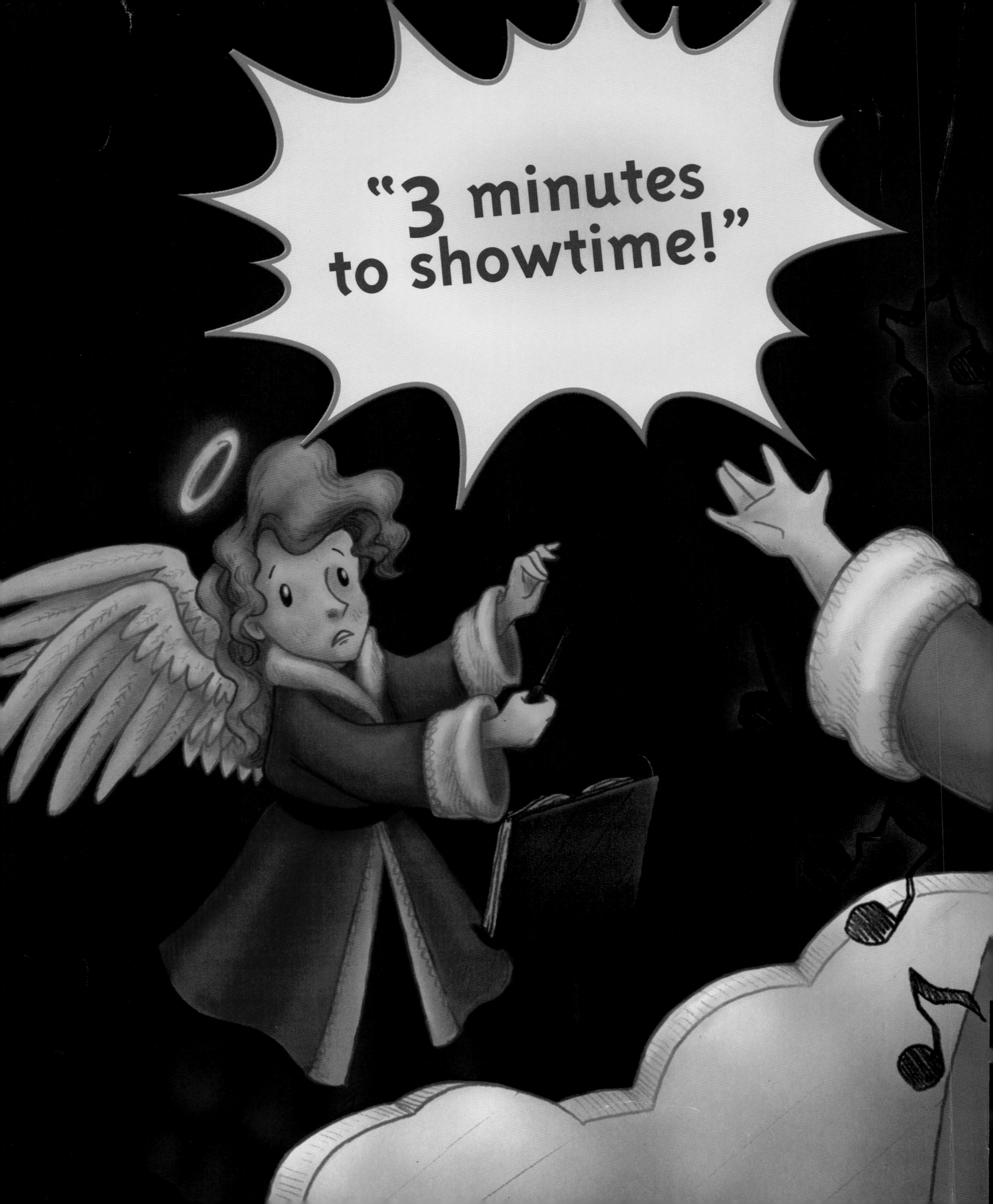
"3 minutes to showtime!"

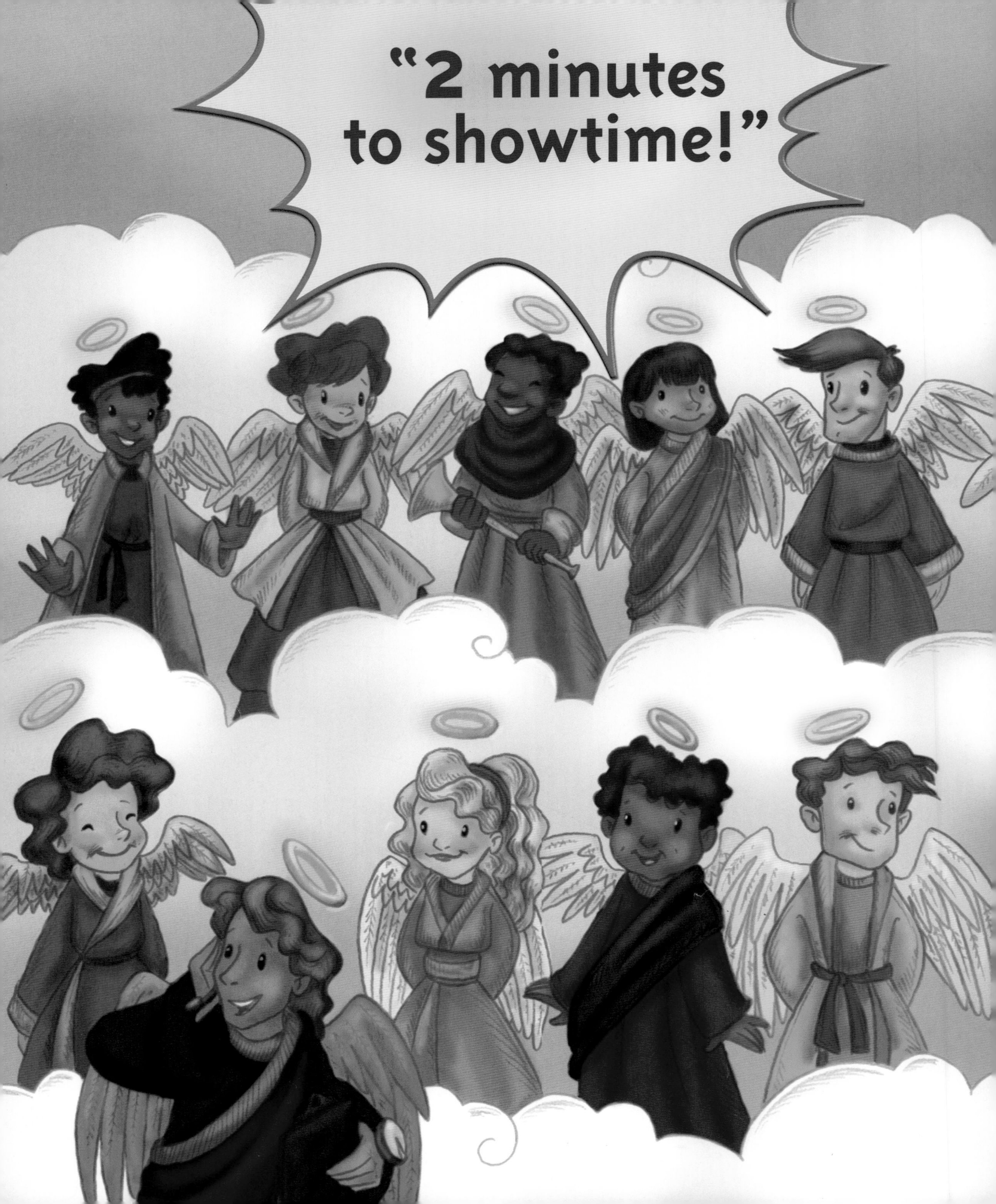
"2 minutes to showtime!"

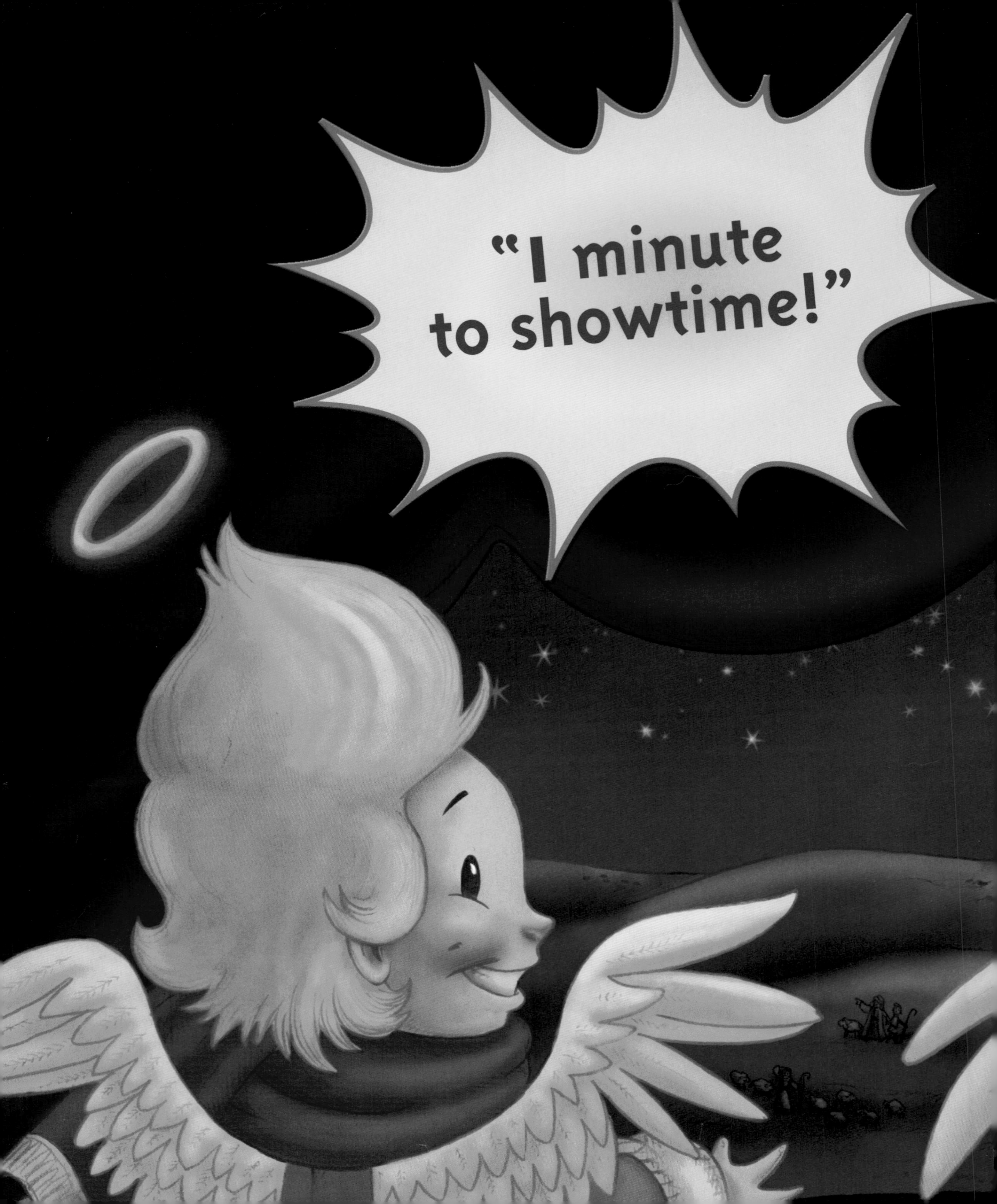
"I minute to showtime!"

" Glory to God in the highest, and o

"He's such a miracle. I sense that all of heaven is rejoicing with us right now."

"I think you're right, my sweets."

"Did you see those chubby cheeks?"

"Did you see all that dark hair sticking out?"

"Wow, he has his father's eyes."